Lee Aucoin, *Creative Director*
Jamey Acosta, *Senior Editor*
Heidi Fiedler, *Editor*
Produced and designed by
Denise Ryan & Associates, Australia
Illustration © Joy Allen
Rachelle Cracchiolo, *Publisher*

Teacher Created Materials
5301 Oceanus Drive
Huntington Beach, CA 92649-1030
http://www.tcmpub.com
Paperback: ISBN: 978-1-4333-5569-1
Library Binding: ISBN: 978-1-4333-1714-5
© 2014 Teacher Created Materials

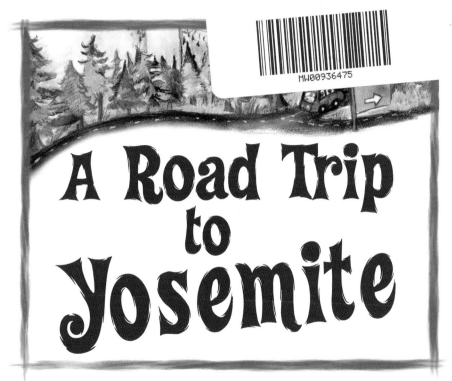

A Road Trip to Yosemite

Written by Helen Bethune

Illustrated by Joy Allen

Amelia fidgeted in the car as her parents finished loading the luggage. The family was going on a road trip to Yosemite National Park for a week.

Amelia was so excited she couldn't sit still. She loved bears. She had read hundreds of books about them.

3

"Dad, can I set the GPS?" Amelia asked, as her father climbed into the driver's seat.

"I've already set it," said Dad.

Her brother Cameron clambered into the car. "We don't need the GPS to go to Yosemite," he said. I read online how a GPS can send you down roads that don't exist."

"But we have to get there first," said Amelia. "It's almost 200 miles from here."

"Okay, gang, let's hit the road," said Dad.

7

"When will we get there?" asked Amelia.

"In about three hours, if we go 65 miles an hour all the way," said Cameron. "But it would be quicker at 80 miles an hour."

"We are NOT speeding," said Dad firmly.

"I know," said Mom. "Let's all guess what time we'll arrive at the lodge. I say four fifteen. Whoever's guess is most off has to do what the person who comes closest says."

9

Dad looked at the GPS. "I'm guessing four o'clock."

Cameron looked at Dad and said, "I say four thirty. You always make a million random stops."

"What if we have a flat?" asked Amelia.

"We won't," said Dad.

11

"What if bears block the road?"

"They won't," said Cameron.

"What if we get lost? What if we end up in Denver?"

"We won't," said Dad. "We've got the GPS, remember?"

"And a map," said Mom. "Tom, don't forget we have to drop by my sister's in Marin County first."

Amelia sighed. "I say six o'clock then."

"First random stop," muttered Cameron.

Finally, after visiting family, they were on Highway 120. The first few dozen miles were straight and narrow. Then, the road climbed into the mountains, becoming windier and prettier. Huge trees lined the road.

CALIFORNIA
120

15

The car rounded curve after curve, and suddenly the family could see across the Yosemite Valley. The afternoon sun lit up the mountains.

Dad pulled the car over to admire the view. "It makes you want to sing 'America the Beautiful,'" he said.

"Come on, Dad, let's go," groaned Amelia. "We won't ever get there if we don't keep driving. I want to see the bears."

"Another random stop," Cameron said. "Told you. I'm going to win."

The road wound down into Yosemite National Park.
Amelia kept watching for bears. Suddenly she said,
"That sign said we should make a right to get to our lodge."

Dad checked the GPS. "No, we keep going straight
along this road."

The road became narrower and rougher as the miles passed. "Tom, are you sure this is the right way?" asked Mom.

"The GPS says so," replied Dad.

"The map doesn't," said Mom, as the road abruptly came to a dead end.

"Huh," said Dad, as he stopped the car. "I guess we better turn back."

Cameron peered at the GPS. "The mountains must have messed up the signal."

Amelia squealed. "Look, look! There's a bear."
As she spoke, a bear rose to its full height and looked toward the car. It was big—very big and very fierce.

For a moment, it stared at the family. Then, it dropped back down on to all fours and disappeared into the darkness of the forest.

"Wow!" everyone said.

"That was AMAZING!" said Amelia happily. "Now, I can say I've seen a bear."

They drove back toward the sign and this time made a left. They reached their lodge just before six o'clock.

Amelia jumped out of the car. "I won! Dad, you were so wrong! The trip took five hours—two hours longer than you said."

"Oh, now I'm in trouble! You get to ask me to do something!"

25

Amelia looked around. Just behind the lodge was a river. "I say you have to see how cold the water is."

"It'll be freezing!" said Dad.

"You don't have to go all the way in," said Amelia kindly. "Just take off your shoes and socks and keep your feet in the water for at least a minute."

Dad sighed and trudged down to the river. Sitting down on the bank, he removed his shoes and socks and quickly plunged his feet into the water.

"Yow!" he yelped. "It's freezing!"

Amelia smiled, "I love road trips, and this one has only just begun."